W9-ATP-385

About the Bank Street Ready-to-Read Series

More than seventy-five years of educational research, innovative teaching, and quality publishing have earned The Bank Street College of Education its reputation as America's most trusted name in early childhood education.

Because no two children are exactly alike in their development, the Bank Street Ready-to-Read series is written on three levels to accommodate the individual stages of reading readiness of children ages three through eight.

- ***Level 1:*** **Getting Ready to Read (Pre-K–Grade 1)**
  Level 1 books are perfect for reading aloud with children who are getting ready to read or just starting to read words or phrases. These books feature large type, repetition, and simple sentences.
- ***Level 2:*** **Reading Together (Grades 1–3)**
  These books have slightly smaller type and longer sentences. They are ideal for children beginning to read by themselves who may need help.
- ***Level 3:*** **I Can Read It Myself (Grades 2–3)**
  These stories are just right for children who can read independently. They offer more complex and challenging stories and sentences.

All three levels of The Bank Street Ready-to-Read books make it easy to select the books most appropriate for your child's development and enable him or her to grow with the series step by step. The levels purposely overlap to reinforce skills and further encourage reading.

We feel that making reading fun is the single most important thing anyone can do to help children become good readers. We hope you will become part of Bank Street's long tradition of learning through sharing.

The Bank Street College of Education

For William and Jonathan Davies
— W.H.H.

For Andrew
— P.M.

For a free color catalog describing Gareth Stevens' list of high-quality books and multimedia programs, call 1-800-542-2595 (USA) or 1-800-461-9120 (Canada). Gareth Stevens Publishing's Fax: (414) 225-0377.
See our catalog, too, on the World Wide Web: http://gsinc.com

Library of Congress Cataloging-in-Publication Data

Hooks, William H.
Mr. Dinosaur / by William H. Hooks; illustrated by Paul Meisel.
p. cm. -- (Bank Street ready-to-read)
Summary: When Eli's fascination with dinosaurs begins to cause him trouble, his older brother finds a clever way to help.
ISBN 0-8368-1755-9 (lib. bdg.)
[1. Brothers--Fiction. 2. Dinosaurs--Fiction. 3. Lizards--Fiction.]
I. Meisel, Paul, ill. II. Title. III. Series.
PZ7.H7664Ms 1997
[E]--dc21 97-1627

This edition first published in 1997 by
Gareth Stevens Publishing
1555 North RiverCenter Drive, Suite 201
Milwaukee, Wisconsin 53212 USA

Printed in Mexico

1 2 3 4 5 6 7 8 9 01 00 99 98 97

Bank Street Ready-to-Read™

Mr. Dinosaur

by William H. Hooks
Illustrated by Paul Meisel

A Byron Preiss Book

Gareth Stevens Publishing
MILWAUKEE

Mr. Dinosaur

My brother Eli is only five years old.
But his best friend is about
a hundred and fifty million years old.
Just ask him "Who is your best friend?"
"Stegosaurus!" he'll shout.
It does no good to tell Eli the last
Stegosaurus was born millions of years ago.
"They live a very long time," he says.

The first time Eli mentioned Stegosaurus,
Mom asked, “Is he in your
kindergarten class?”
I thought Mom was joking.
She wasn’t.
She’s just not into dinosaurs.
Me neither.

Eli is a walking dictionary of dinosaurs.
He still says *pist-getti* for *spaghetti.*
But he has no trouble
with long dinosaur names
like Diplodocus and Tyrannosaurus rex.
I tease him by calling him Mr. Dinosaur.
Does he mind?
He loves it!

Meat Eaters and Plant Eaters

Mr. Dinosaur has a big collection of
his favorite animals—all dinosaurs.
He keeps them on two tables in our room.
One day my friend Roberta bumped
into the tables.
Some of the dinosaurs fell on the floor.
We were putting them back
just as Eli walked in.

"Help!" screamed Mr. Dinosaur.
"What's wrong?" asked Roberta.
"Stegosaurus is in danger!" he shouted.
"What kind of danger?" I asked.
"You put Tyrannosaurus rex on the table with the plant eaters," he cried.

Eli grabbed Tyrannosaurus rex.
"This big-tooth monster will eat
my friend Steggie," he said.
"Why doesn't Steggie bite him back?"
asked Roberta.
"Because," said Mr. Dinosaur,
"Stegosaurus is a friendly plant eater."

"You sure know a lot about dead animals,"
said Roberta.
"They're not *all* dead," answered Eli.
"Come on, Mr. Dinosaur," I said. "All
the dinosaurs died millions of years ago."
"Uh-uh," he said. "I see them on TV."
"Oh, that's just make-believe,"
said Roberta. "Cartoons are not real."
"They're *not* cartoons," said Eli.
"They're really real.
There's a terrible meat-eating
Tyrannosaurus rex on *Lost in Time*."

Eli rushed out of the room
with his Stegosaurus.
"Oh, brother," said Roberta. "I see
trouble with Mr. Dinosaur."
Roberta was right.

That night Eli took Stegosaurus to bed.
“OK, Steggie,” he whispered.
“You stay under the covers in case
one of those meat eaters gets hungry.”
He was still talking to Steggie
when I fell asleep.

Suddenly I was wide awake.
"Help! Help!"
Eli was screaming in the dark.
"What's wrong?" I asked.
"Steggie is in trouble!" he yelled.
"Tyrannosaurus rex is chasing
Stegosaurus and Diplodocus!"

The light went on in our room.
"What's going on?" asked Mom.
There was Eli standing in the middle
of the room shouting "Stop!"
I could see he was having a nightmare.
Mom shook him and said, "Eli, wake up!"

He opened his eyes and said, “Thanks, Mom.
Thanks for helping me save Steggie.”
“It was only a dream,” said Mom.
“Come back to bed.”
Mom sat with him till he fell asleep.

When Mom left, she whispered to me,
"It's just a phase Eli's going through.
You get some sleep now."
As I drifted off to sleep, I was thinking,
"I hope this phase won't last
a million years, Mr. Dinosaur."

The Lizard and the Egg

The next day Roberta came over.
She was carrying a box with holes
punched in it.
"Surprise!" she cried.
"Guess what I have."

“A gerbil!” I said.
“No, guess again,” she said.
“A guinea pig?”
“No, one more guess.”
“A baby dinosaur,” I said.
“Close,” said Roberta.
She lifted the lid.
A green lizard stuck out his tongue at me.
“Ugh,” said Roberta. “Gross, isn’t it?
My uncle gave it to me.”

"What are you going to do with him?"
I asked.
"It's a her," said Roberta.
"Do you think Eli would like her?"
"She does look a lot like a little
dinosaur," I said.
"He'll *love* her."

Just then we heard a loud yell
from behind the house.
We ran to the window.
Eli was in the backyard
jumping up and down
and shouting like crazy.

Roberta and I ran outside.
The backyard was all dug up.
There were holes everywhere.
Eli was covered with dirt.
“Look! Look!” he shouted.
He pointed a shovel at a big rock.
“A dinosaur egg!” he yelled.
“I found a real dinosaur egg!”
“Looks like a rock to me,” said Roberta.
“No! It’s a dinosaur egg,” he cried.
He lifted the big round rock
and staggered toward the house with it.

“The lizard!” cried Roberta.
“I left the lid off the box!”
We raced past Eli into the house.
The box was empty.
We quickly searched the house.
No lizard.

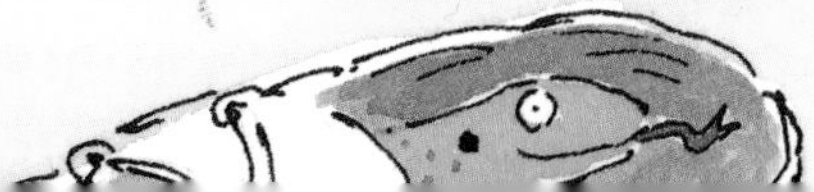

Eli took the rock
straight to the empty box.
"This will make a good nest
for my dinosaur egg," he said.
Roberta elbowed me and whispered,
"Mum's the word on the lizard."

Eli pushed the box near the radiator.
“I’ve got to keep my egg warm
so it will hatch,” he explained.
I was busy wondering where
the lizard was.
“Whatever you say, Mr. Dinosaur,” I sighed.

Eli folded his arms across his chest.
Then he looked at me and Roberta.
"My egg's going to hatch," he said.
"Just wait and see!"

The New Baby

I looked for the lizard all week.
Finally I gave up and called Roberta.
"I think I've solved the mystery
of the missing lizard," I said.
"Tell me," said Roberta.

"Lizards like water, right?" I asked.
"Sure," said Roberta.
"Well, I think the lizard escaped down the bathtub drain."
Roberta laughed.
"Don't laugh," I said.
"I've heard of baby alligators going down the drain. Why not lizards?"
"You could be right," said Roberta.
"What's up with Eli and the big egg?"

“Eli takes that rock to bed at night
to keep it warm.”
“Oh, brother,” said Roberta.
“Mom says this is going on too long,
and Eli is in for a big disappointment.”

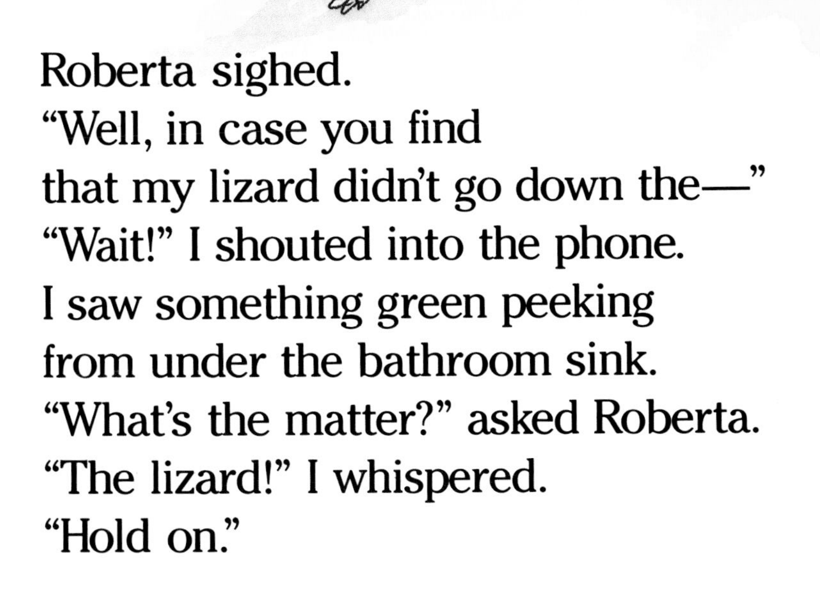

Roberta sighed.
“Well, in case you find
that my lizard didn’t go down the—”
“Wait!” I shouted into the phone.
I saw something green peeking
from under the bathroom sink.
“What’s the matter?” asked Roberta.
“The lizard!” I whispered.
“Hold on.”

I tiptoed into the bathroom.
Holding my empty laundry bag
in one hand, I scooped up the lizard
and dropped her in.
Then I rushed back to the phone.
"Hello! You still there?"
"What's going on?" cried Roberta.
"The lizard! I've got her!" I shouted.
"Listen," said Roberta.
"I've got a great idea.
Hold on to that lizard.
I'm coming right over."

Roberta was there in five minutes.
“Where’s Eli?” she asked.
“At the store with Mom,” I said.
“Great,” said Roberta.
“We have to move fast.
Where’s the lizard?”
“In the laundry bag,” I said.
“Come on,” said Roberta.
“Eli’s egg is about to hatch!”

We dumped the rock out of the box
and put the lizard inside.
"What about eggshells?" I asked.
"Eli's smart. He'll wonder what
happened to the shell."
"I thought of that," said Roberta,
opening the paper bag she brought.
She put pieces of brown eggshell in the box.

Then we took Mr. Dinosaur's egg to the backyard and put it back in its resting place.

By the time we finished, Mom and Eli
were coming in the front door.
Eli ran straight to his room
to check on his egg.

"Wow!" we heard him yell.
"I told you so!"
"What?" called Mom from the kitchen.
"It hatched," cried Eli.
"I've got a baby dinosaur!"
We all ran to look.
Eli was holding the box
and stroking the green lizard.
Mom looked puzzled.
I winked at her.
Roberta whispered, "Shh!"

"She's beautiful," said Eli.
"I'm naming her Dippy, for Diplodocus."
"How did he know it was a *her*?"
asked Roberta.
"Eli is smart," I admitted.

After a couple of weeks Roberta
and I told Eli about the lizard.
By then he was so fond of Dippy that
it didn't matter.
Like Mom said, dinosaurs were just
a phase for Eli.
I think she's right.
And I think I know
what his next phase will be—
real, live lizards!

William H. Hooks is the author of many books for children, including the highly acclaimed *Moss Gown*. As part of Bank Street's Media Group, he has been closely involved with such projects as the well-known Bank Street Readers and Discoveries:
An Individualized Reading Program. Mr. Hooks lives with three cats in North Carolina.

Paul Meisel was graduated from the Yale School of Art and worked as an art director before becoming a full-time illustrator. He is a frequent contributor to the *New York Times* and the illustrator of *Monkey-Monkey's Trick*. Mr. Meisel lives with his wife and three sons in Newtown, Connecticut.